MONSTER BUDDIES

I'M FROM OUTER SPACE!

MEET AN ALIEN

Lisa Bullard

illustrated by Mike Moran

MILLBROOK PRESS • MINNEAPOLIS

For Wendy –LB

Millbrook Press
A division of Lerner Publishing Group, Inc.
241 First Avenue North
Minneapolis, MN 55401 USA

For reading levels and more information, look up this title at www.lernerbooks.com.

Main body text set in Sunshine Regular 17/24.
Typeface provided by Chank.

Library of Congress Cataloging-in-Publication Data

Bullard, Lisa.
    I'm from outer space! Meet an alien / by Lisa Bullard ; illustrated by Mike Moran.
        pages   cm. — (Monster buddies)
    ISBN 978-0-7613-9193-7 (lib. bdg. : alk. paper)
    ISBN 978-1-4677-4782-0 (eBook)
    1. Extraterrestrial beings—Juvenile literature. 2. Unidentified flying objects—
Juvenile literature. I. Moran, Michael, 1957– illustrator. II. Title.
TL789.2.B85 2015
001.942—dc23   2013038927

Manufactured in the United States of America
1 – BOL – 7/15/14

TABLE OF CONTENTS

Greetings, Earthling

Greetings, Earthling. Could you step closer? I'd like to hook you up to this machine. It helps me study creatures all over the universe.

My name is Zeeton. I'm an alien. Aliens are beings who come from outer space. I'm from the planet Pongo. I flew here on a spaceship. Someday soon I might take over your world!

Bossy Big Brain

Don't gather friends to fight me off! Alien monsters have never flown to Earth. You and your planet are safe.

You'll see strange photos of spaceships in the sky. You'll hear stories about people meeting aliens on dark nights. And you'll see aliens in movies and on TV. But those monsters are make-believe. The photos and the stories aren't real.

I have green skin and big, dark eyes. My body is small and weak. You probably think that you could beat me in arm wrestling.

But my brain is much bigger than yours! I'm very smart. I have special powers. I can make you do whatever I want you to.

My friends and I have lived on the planet Pongo for a long time. But Pongo is getting crowded. So we built spaceships. We fly from one planet to another.

We're looking for a new home.

The ship I travel on is flat and round. It has colorful blinking lights. It's much faster than your fastest rocket. Your people call it a flying saucer or an unidentified flying object (UFO).

We've visited Earth many times. We fly in at night. We land in a dark place. Then we take people or animals onto our spaceship.

Think of us as doctors. We do tests on Earth
creatures. The tests tell us if we could live on your
planet. Last trip, we studied one of those animals
you call a cow.

See this mark? She kicked me!

So far, I like what I see on Earth. I especially like these things you call puppies. And bubble gum! You can't get that in space.

I want to keep doing tests until we figure out how to stay here. Maybe someday I'll be your neighbor! As long as you follow my orders, it will work out fine.

Friend or Foe?

People on Earth have talked about aliens for thousands of years. How did the stories get started? People probably saw strange things in the sky. Modern scientists could explain these sights. They know a comet when they see one. But back then, people didn't have answers.

Reports of UFOs still come from all around the world. Often the UFO turns out to be someone playing a joke. Sometimes, a person mistakes an airplane for an alien ship.

All sorts of aliens star in Earth's books and movies. I've met some oddball aliens on my travels too. My friends come from different planets. Ishtoo is green. Pretta looks like you. But Ippo is like a giant lizard with tiger teeth and claws!

Some aliens are friendly, like the one in the movie
E.T. But don't invite Ippo over for dinner.

He'd rather make you his meal!

Time for a Quick Test

When you look up at the sky, don't worry. I won't beam you up into my ship. I won't hook you up to machines.

Because aliens have never landed on Earth. Of course, you're a very interesting Earthling. If I were real, I'd just love to study you! Could you hold this for a minute? I want to run one more test!

An Alien's Day Writing Activity

You've learned a lot about aliens. Now it's time to have some out-of-this-world fun. Grab a pencil and a piece of paper. Write a short story about a day in the life of an alien. What happens when your alien meets someone from a different planet? Do aliens have to eat their vegetables? Draw a picture to go with your story.

GLOSSARY

creatures: living beings

Earthling: a name that aliens often call Earth people in stories

saucer: a round, almost flat dish

spaceship: a flying machine that carries someone through space

UFO: unidentified flying object, or something in the sky that cannot be explained

universe: everything that exists in space

TO LEARN MORE

Books

Brecke, Nicole, and Patricia M. Stockland. *Spaceships, Aliens, and Robots You Can Draw.*
Minneapolis: Millbrook Press, 2010.
This book shows readers how to draw creepy creatures and cool ships from alien stories.

Hughes, Catherine D. *First Big Book of Space.* Washington, DC: National Geographic, 2012.
Check out this book to learn about stars, planets, and space travel.

Websites

KidsAstronomy
http://www.kidsastronomy.com/
Take a trip to this website to play games and learn more about space.

NASA Kids' Club
http://www.nasa.gov/audience/forkids/kidsclub/flash/#.Uj8-rRAQPjK
This site from the National Aeronautics and Space Administration has video footage, games, and articles for students.

INDEX